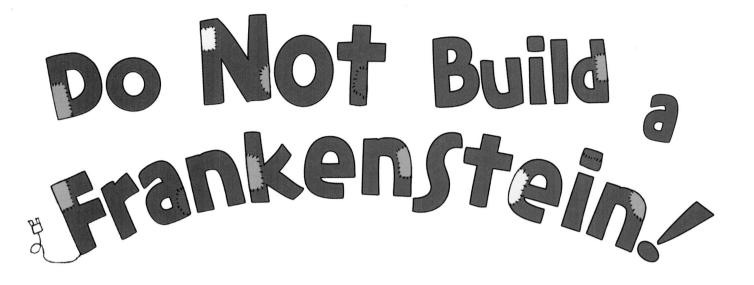

Do Not Build a Frankenstein!

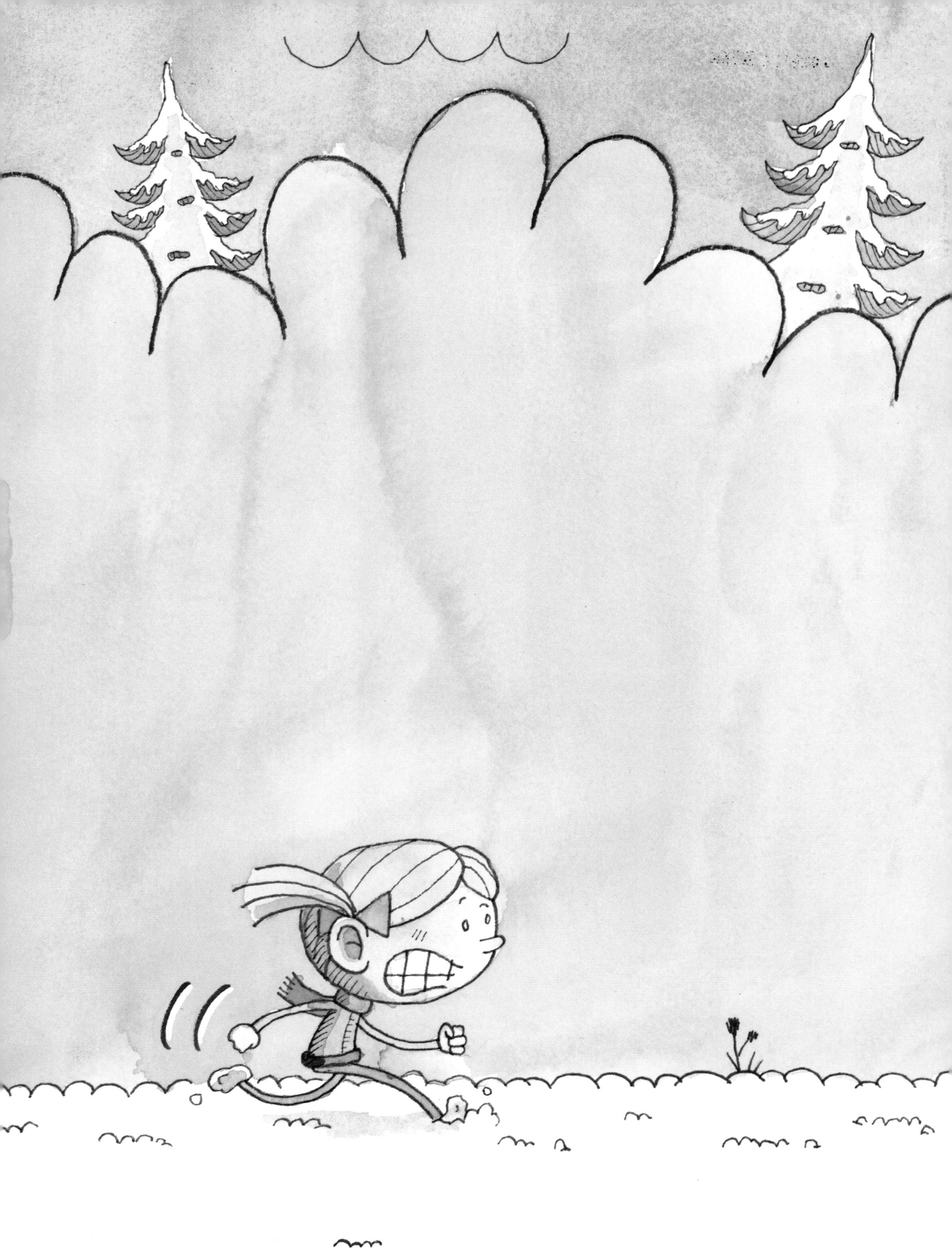

Do Not Build a Frankenstein!

by Neil Numberman

Greenwillow Books

An Imprint of HarperCollinsPublishers

Do Not Build a Frankenstein!
Copyright © 2009 by Neil Numberman
All rights reserved. Manufactured in China.
For information address HarperCollins Children's
Books, a division of HarperCollins Publishers,
10 East 53rd Street, New York, NY 10022.
www.harpercollinschildrens.com

Watercolors were used to prepare the full-color art.
The text type is Martin Gothic.

Library of Congress Cataloging-in-Publication Data
Numberman, Neil.
Do not build a Frankenstein! / by Neil Numberman.
p. cm.
"Greenwillow Books."
Summary: A boy warns his new neighbors of the trouble that comes
with building a monster, including having to move to a different town
in hopes of escaping his creation.
ISBN 978-0-06-156816-9 (trade bdg.) — ISBN 978-0-06-156817-6 (lib. bdg.)
[1. Monsters—Fiction. 2. Moving, Household—Fiction.] I. Title.
PZ7.N96356Do 2009   [E]—dc22   2008020751

First Edition 09 10 11 12 13 SCP 10 9 8 7 6 5 4 3 2 1

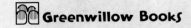 Greenwillow Books

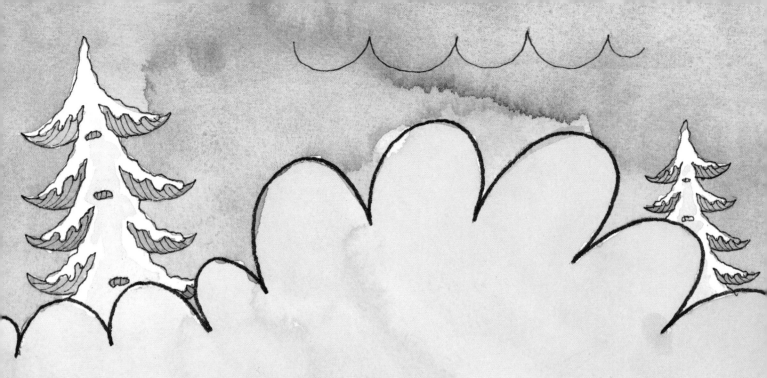

To Ryan and Connor,
the Frankenfamily

Gather round! Gather round!
I have very important advice to give!

Trust me. I know. I tried.
You must dedicate your entire life
to building a Frankenstein.

You must research . . .

build a laboratory . . .

and find the right parts.

At first, having a Frankenstein may be fun.

But after a while . . .

it can become pretty annoying.

He'll chase away your friends . . .

and your pets . . .

and he'll break all your toys.

and pretend that he's not.

Even when you try to ignore him,
he keeps bothering you.

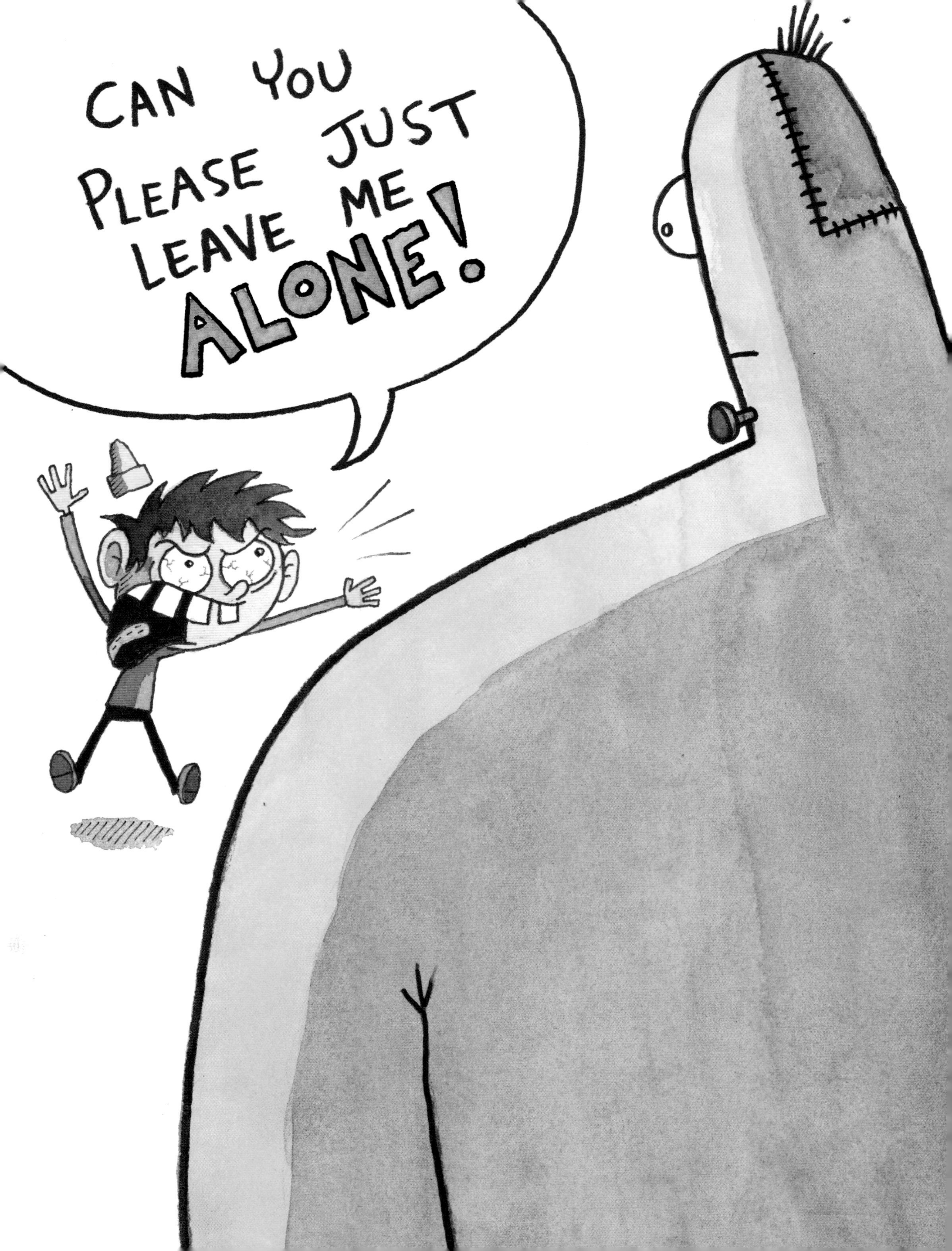
CAN YOU PLEASE JUST LEAVE ME ALONE!

All you can do is move away,
to a new town full of new people.

So friends, I'm begging you.
Take my advice . . .